# The Mum-Minder

## Jacqueline Wilson

## Illustrated by Nick Sharratt

CORGI YEARLING

THE MUM-MINDER
A CORGI YEARLING BOOK 978 0 440 86825 5

First published in Great Britain by Doubleday,
an imprint of Random House Children's Books
A Random House Group Company

Doubleday edition published 1993
First Corgi Yearling edition published 1994
This Corgi Yearling edition published 2008

9 10 8

The Random House Group Limited supports The Forest Stewardship Council (FSC®), the
leading international forest certification organisation. Our books carrying the FSC label are
printed on FSC® certified paper. FSC is the only forest certification scheme endorsed by the
leading environmental organisations, including Greenpeace. Our paper procurement policy
can be found at www.randomhouse.co.uk/environment

MIX
Paper from
responsible sources
FSC® C016897

Corgi Yearling Books are published by Random House Children's Books,
61–63 Uxbridge Road, London W5 5SA

www.kidsatrandomhouse.co.uk

Addresses for companies within The Random House Group Limited can be found at:
www.randomhouse.co.uk/offices.htm

THE RANDOM HOUSE GROUP Limited Reg. No. 954009

A CIP catalogue record for this book is available from the British Library.

Printed and bound by CPI Group (UK) Ltd, Croydon, CR0 4YY

*For the Dimwits who aren't dim at all,*
*but are very witty*

It's half-term. No more stupid, boring, silly old school for a whole week!

Oh-oh. Maybe that's not tactful seeing as this is a school project. We've all got to keep a holiday diary. I've got to hand this in next Monday. I can't rub it out because it's written with my mum's biro and it would just make great blue smears all over the page. My baby sister Sara chewed my own pen up yesterday. My special red felt-tip pen which also doubles as a lipstick if I'm dressing up. Sara's not

got all her teeth yet but she can't half chew. She looked like Dracula with all this red ink dripping down her chin.

I felt really cross with her but that's babies for you. I get more than a bit fed up with babies sometimes. I am surrounded by them right this minute. Three-year-old Gemma

keeps pulling at my arm, wanting me to draw for her. Two-year-old Vincent is drawing himself, making horrible scribbles on the back of a paper bag. Baby Clive is having a yell because Mum's put him down for a nap and he doesn't feel like it. And Sara's sitting on my foot, bouncing up and down, wanting a ride.

They're not all my brothers and sisters. No fear. My sister Sara's quite enough to be going on with.

No, my mum's a childminder. She doesn't have to mind me. I'm Sadie and I'm nearly nine. I can mind myself, easy-peasy. I can look after Sara too. I sometimes get up in the night and give her a bottle. And I play with her and I take her out for a walk in her pushchair. I do a lot of things for my mum and all. I make her a cup of tea when she's tired and I've got this knack of massaging her feet which she loves.

'I don't know what I'd do without you, Sadie,' she says.

We don't see much of my dad nowa-
days, but it doesn't matter.

'Us girls will stick together, eh?'
says Mum, and sometimes I climb up
on her lap as well as Sara and we all
have a big hug together.

I quite like my mum being a child-minder because she's always there when I get home from school. The only trouble is in the holidays. Babies don't have holidays. They don't have half-terms either. Mum gets lumbered with them all the time.

If it was just Mum and me then this half-term would be great. We could go down to the shops and look round at all the clothes and the toys and choose what we'd buy if we had all the money in the world. Or we could go to the Leisure Centre and have a swim in the pool. They've got a big wave machine and all my friends say it's smashing. Or we could play that I'm a lady too and we could go and have a pot of tea and a Danish pastry each and have a good gossip in a proper restaurant. But you can't go shopping or swimming or eating when you've got four babies. My sister Sara would be bad enough. But if we've got Gemma and

Vincent and little Clive as well then it's impossible.

Nan usually helps. She acts as Mum's assistant. She's got another job working in a pub at nights but she doesn't mind giving Mum a hand too. You need lots and lots of hands with all those babies. But Nan phoned up this morning and said she couldn't make it. Grandad's off work with the flu. My grandad's like a great big baby himself. Nan's going to be busy looking after him for a few days.

'Never mind, Mum. *I'll* be your assistant,' I said. 'Good job I'm off school, eh?'

So I've done my best. It hasn't been easy. Especially when we went out for a walk and called in at the corner shop. Mum uses a double buggy and I carried Sara but it was still a job carting them around. And then Sara started shrieking in the shop because she wanted Smarties, and Gemma picked a packet of jelly off the shelf

and wouldn't let go, and Vincent went rushing round the corner and barged straight into a pile of toilet rolls and knocked them all over the place, and Clive yelled his head off all the time.

He's been yelling all day. It doesn't half get on your nerves. It's given Mum a headache. She looks ever so white and tired. Hang on. I know what I'll do.


*Later*
Well I've made Mum a cup of tea. She's had a couple of aspirins too, though they don't look as if they're helping much. I've given Clive another bottle and he's got off to

sleep. I've sat on the sofa with the others and read them this story about Dominic the Vole. Dominic the Vole is fat and funny and he's always getting into trouble. (Very like my little sister Sara.) Gemma liked the story and wanted me to read it again, but Vincent got fidgety and Sara kept wanting to hold the book herself but when I let her she bit right into it. Dominic the Vole has got teethmarks across his bottom now.

'You're being the childminder today, Sadie,' Mum said. 'I'd better give you half my wages.'

'Are you feeling better now, Mum?'

'Yes,' said Mum, but she didn't sound sure. She sneezed suddenly.

'You sound as if you're getting a cold, Mum,' I said.

'No I'm not,' said Mum, and then she sneezed again. She blew her nose. 'Just a little sniffle, that's all. I'm OK. I'll take over the kids now, Sadie. You can go out and play.'

*Later still*

I had a good game with my friend Rachel up the road, but I kept looking in on Mum. She looked whiter than ever and she was shivering. The babies were all being very boisterous. I knew Mum was longing to get shot of them all. Well, she's got to put up with Sara all the time, but that can't be helped.

Clive's mum usually comes first because her chocolate shop closes at half-past five. But she's going to a babywear party tonight so she asked

Mum to have him for the whole evening. And then Vincent's mum rang up and said the trains were up the spout and she'd be late getting back from the office to pick him up. And then, to crown it all, Gemma's mum phoned to say she'd arrested someone – she's a policewoman, you see – and she'd probably be an hour or so later than planned.

'That's OK,' Mum said to Clive's mum and Vincent's mum and Gemma's mum.

'But you don't feel well, Mum,' I said.

'Us girls have got to stick together,' said Mum.

So she looked after all the babies. I put Sara to bed and then, by the time we'd got rid of Vincent and Gemma and at long last Clive, Mum said she felt so shattered she wanted to go to bed too.

She was so tired I had to help her undress and then I tucked her up under the covers and gave her a kiss.

'You're being a mum-minder now,'
said Mum.

We didn't get off to a good start today. Sara was awake half the night and Mum had to keep getting up to her. So she was so tired she slept right through her alarm and we didn't wake up until Vincent's mum rang the doorbell.

'Oh no,' said Mum.

Something seemed to have happened to her voice overnight. She sounded more like my dad than my mum.

She stumbled downstairs in her

nightie, croaking to me to put the kettle on. Sara started yelling for attention so I put my head round her door.

'Ook,' she said proudly.

She was standing up in her cot, hanging on to the rail, bouncing her fat little feet. She'd managed to unpop her pyjamas *and* her nappy. She suddenly stood still and started weeing, a look of wonder on her face.

'Sara!' I shouted, and snatched her out of the cot but I was several seconds too late. It looked like the whole of Sara's bedding was going to have to go in the washing machine.

'You're a bad girl. Poor Mum's feeling rotten and you're just making things worse for her,' I said severely.

'Yup,' said Sara, and giggled.

I bundled her under one arm and went downstairs to see to the kettle. Vincent's mum was in the kitchen, stalking about in her high heels, looking a bit tetchy because we were in such a muddle. She was holding

Vincent warily, not wanting him to dribble down her smart suit. Vincent is getting a back tooth and has turned into a human waterfall.

'Sorry I overslept,' Mum mumbled. 'Here, I'll take Vincent. You get off to work now, you don't want to be late.'

'Yes, well, I have got this very important meeting this morning,' said Vincent's mum, but she looked

at my mum a bit worriedly. 'Are you all right? You don't look very well,' she said, absent-mindedly slotting Vincent into the highchair in the kitchen.

Sara started shrieking indignantly in my arms. It's her highchair and she doesn't care to share it. Vincent started shouting too because his mum wasn't watching what she was doing and was bending one of his legs backwards.

'I'm fine,' said Mum, unhooking Vincent's leg and taking the struggling Sara from me.

'You don't *look* fine,' said Vincent's mum.

'I've just got a little sniffle, that's all,' said Mum.

Vincent's mum didn't look convinced, but she had her important meeting so she whisked off sharpish.

Mum let Sara slide off her lap and rested her head in her arms.

'I think you'd better go back to bed, Mum,' I said.

'No, I'm OK, love, really,' said Mum. 'Well, I will be when I've had a nice cup of tea.'

Gemma and her mum turned up while we were still having breakfast. Gemma's mum let me try on her police hat while she had a cup of tea too. I frisked Gemma and cautioned Vincent and made some handcuffs

out of tinfoil and captured Sara but she simply chewed her way free.

Mum had two cups of tea and said she felt much better. She didn't look better at all. She was white with black rings round her eyes, just like Sara's toy panda.

She was still sneezing.

'Sorry about my cold,' Mum sniffed. 'I'll try not to give it to the kids.'

'You sound as if you've got a bit more than a cold,' said Gemma's mum. 'I feel a bit mean leaving you to cope, especially as your mum can't come. But I've got to go to court this morning, so I've really got to leave Gemma with you.'

'That's all right. We'll manage, don't worry,' said Mum, and she looked at me.

I sighed. It looked like I was going to be reading *Dominic the Vole* until I was blue in the face.

Gemma's mum pushed off and Mum crawled away to get washed and dressed. She tried putting on a

bit of make-up so that she didn't look so bad, but it just looked weird – white face, black eyes and bright red lipstick. Mum's nose was getting red to match because she was having to wipe it so often.

'It's just a little cold. I won't breathe on the baby,' Mum told Clive's mum.

'I think my Clive's got a bit of a cold himself,' said Clive's mum. 'He's in a bit of a bad mood today. Got the grizzles and won't stop.'

'Oh,' said Mum weakly, and rubbed her forehead.

'Have you got a headache?' said Clive's mum.

'Just a bit,' said Mum.

'Are you sure you haven't got flu?' said Clive's mum. 'There's a lot of it about.'

'No, no,' said Mum. 'Of course I haven't.'

Clive's mum went off to her chocolate shop and we were left with all the babies.

'Don't worry, I'll give you a hand, Mum,' I said, but then my friend Rachel from up the road came round to see if I wanted to go over to her house to watch videos.

'I can't really. I've got to help my mum because she's not feeling well,' I said.

'I'm feeling fine,' Mum said determinedly. 'You go round to Rachel's and have a bit of fun, Sadie.'

So I did. Rachel and I watched a Walt Disney video and then her dad

went out to do the shopping and we watched this really scary monster video instead, fast forwarding through the worst bits. Then we took turns being the Monster Blob and obliterating each other, and I was having such good fun I forgot all about Mum and the Monster Blobby Babies.

I was very late getting back. And oh dear. Clive was in his carrycot, bellowing fit to bust. Gemma had the television turned up too loud and was fiddling with the knobs to make it even louder. Vincent was crayoning all over the wall with Mum's red lipstick. Sara had chewed an entire corner off the *Dominic the Vole* book so that his little snout and one whole paw were missing. And Mum was sitting in the middle of the floor with great big tears running down her cheeks.

'I don't think I am fine after all,' she sobbed. 'And I phoned Nan to see if she can take over tomorrow

but Grandad's really bad and she's
starting to sneeze all over the place
herself.'

I felt ever so ever so ever so mean. I
hadn't helped Mum one little bit.

Gemma's mum finished at court
early and came round to see how
Mum was.

She took one look and shook her
head.

'You've definitely got flu. Go on up to bed this instant. I'll look after the kids until the other mums get here. Sadie will help me, won't you, pal?'

'Yes, of course.'

'Well, all right then,' Mum groaned. 'But I'll be better tomorrow, I promise.'

'That's nonsense,' said Gemma's mum. 'You'll have to take to your bed and stay there.'

'But what about the babies?' said Mum, sniffling.

'We'll sort something out, won't we, Sadie?' said Gemma's mum.

'You bet,' I said. 'Us girls have got to stick together.'

# WEDNESDAY

You'll never guess what! I've been a *real* policewoman today. Gemma's mum took me to work with her. And her Gemma. And our Sara. And Vincent and little Clive. All of us.

My Mum has got flu. Gemma's mum drove her to the doctor's last night. Mum's got to stay in bed today and tomorrow and the next day. So has Nan. She's got it too.

'I can't have flu. I'm never ill,' Mum moaned. 'I can't let you all down. I've got to look after the kids.'

'Well, you *are* ill, whether we like it or not,' said Gemma's mum. 'And you've never let us down before. You've always looked after our kids. So we've got to stick together, like Sadie said.'

'That's right. And it's OK. *I'll* look after the babies,' I said. I was feeling bad about leaving Mum to cope on her own and I was desperate to make up for it.

'It's sweet of you to offer, Sadie, but you're only a kid yourself, love,' said Gemma's mum.

I got a bit annoyed at that. I'm not a kid, I'm nearly nine for goodness sake, and Mum says I'm old for my age. I look after Sara enough times. If you can cope with our Sara then other babies are a doddle. Gemma's quite a sensible little kid at times, and Vincent's OK if you keep an eye on him – well, two eyes plus one in the back of your head – and baby Clive doesn't yell *all* the time.

But Gemma's mum and Vincent's

mum and Clive's mum and even *my* mum wouldn't listen to me. They said I couldn't cope.

'We're the ones who are going to have to cope,' said Gemma's mum.

'But how?' said Vincent's mum. 'I can't leave Vincent with a neighbour because they go out to work too.'

'My mother-in-law always said she'd look after any babies if I had to go back to work, but the first time she looked after Clive he cried all the time and she said Never Again,' said Clive's mum. 'She just couldn't manage.'

'We're going to have to manage,'

said Gemma's mum. 'It's only for this week. Can't anyone take three days off work? I would, but I've used up all my leave.'

Vincent's mum and Clive's mum couldn't take time off either.

'Then just this once we'll have to take the kids to work with us,' said Gemma's mum.

'How on earth could I have the babies in my office?' said Vincent's mum.

'You can't have kids cooped up behind the chocolate counter all day,' said Clive's mum.

'I'll look after them as usual,' my mum croaked. 'I can go to bed when they have their naps and —'

'Nonsense,' said Gemma's mum. 'Now listen. Tomorrow *I'll* have the kids. They can come to the police station with me. Then Thursday they can go uptown to your office and Friday go to the shop. I know it's going to be difficult but we'll just have to give it a whirl.'

I still feel like I'm whirling. And it's great great great!

I got up ever so early and gave Sara a baby bottle to keep her quiet while I got washed and dressed, and then I made Mum a cup of tea and some toast for her breakfast. Then I heated up some tomato soup at the same time and poured it into a vacuum flask.

'That's your lunch, Mum,' I explained, when I'd woken her and propped a couple of pillows behind her. 'And look, I've brought some

apples and biscuits up, and the kettle
and the coffee and Sara's Ribena
because I think you need the vitamin
C more than she does.'

'You're a real pal, Sadie,' Mum
mumbled. 'So where are you going
today then? Round to Rachel's?'

'You must be joking! I'll have to go
to the police station with Gemma's
mum. She'll never cope with the
babies on her own.'

You can say that again.

She looked a bit fussed when she
came to pick us up.

'Me and my big mouth,' she said. 'I haven't a clue what my boss is going to say. I don't *think* there's anything in Police Orders about not bringing your children and all their little friends to work with you, but I kind of get the feeling it's going to be frowned on.'

Gemma's mum's Police Inspector boss did frown when he saw all of us. His eyebrows practically knitted together.

'What on earth are you playing at, WPC Parsons?' he said.

'Oh, Sir,' said Gemma's mum, and she started gabbling this long, involved, apologetic explanation,

while Gemma scuffed her shoes and Vincent picked his nose and Sara struggled in my arms and Clive cried in his carrycot.

'This is ridiculous,' said the Inspector. 'You're a policewoman, not Mary Blooming Poppins. I can't have my police station turned into a nursery, not even for one day. You must take them all home with you right this minute.'

Sara had stopped struggling. She was staring up at the Inspector. Then she gave him a big sunny smile.

'Dad-Dad!' she announced delightedly.

The Inspector looked shocked.

'I'm not your Dad-Dad,' he said.

'*Dad-Dad!*' Sara insisted, and held out her chubby arms to him.

It's not her fault. We don't often see our dad. Sara's only little and she makes mistakes.

The Inspector was big and he looked as if he'd never made a mistake in his life – but he made one

right that minute. His arms reached out of their own accord. Sara snuggled up to him happily.

'Dad-Dad,' she announced smugly, patting his cheek.

He still tried to frown, but he couldn't stop his mouth going all smiley.

'Is this your little girl, WPC Parsons?' he asked.

'No, Sir. This one's mine. Gemma. Say hello to the Inspector, Gemma,' said Gemma's mum.

Gemma wasn't going to let Sara get all the attention. She smiled determinedly at the Inspector, tossing her curls.

'Hello, Mr Inspector Man. I've come to work with Mummy.'

'Well. Just for today,' said the Inspector, picking her up too.

Gemma's mum winked at me. It looked like it was going to be OK after all.

'How would you like a ride in my police car, eh?' said the Inspector.

'Me too, me too, me too!' said Vincent, tugging at the Inspector's trouser leg.

Clive let out a long, loud wail from his carrycot.

'He's practising being a police siren,' I said.

The Inspector looked at me.

'You're not one of the babies,' he said.

'I should think not,' I said indignantly. 'I'm here to keep them all in order.'

'I'm glad to hear it. It looks as if it's going to be some undertaking,' said the Inspector. 'We'd better give you a bit of authority.'

He found me a policewoman's hat and a special tie and a big badge.

'There we go. Now you're head of my Child Protection Team. What's your name?'

'Sadie. Sir,' I added, and I gave him a little salute.

'I'm glad you've reported for duty, WPC Sadie,' he said. 'Right, I'll give you your orders. Quieten the baby. Wipe the little boy's nose – my trousers are getting rather damp. And take these two little treasures from me so I can give you a proper salute back.'

Gemma jumped down happily enough but Sara screamed when I tried to take her.

'Dad-Dad!' she insisted furiously — and that poor nice-after-all Inspector had to carry her around all day long.

We had a wonderful time. The Inspector really did take us out in a big police car. He wouldn't go very fast but he did put the siren on

just for a second. That was another mistake. Vincent made very loud police-siren noises all day after that, and Clive did his best to accompany him.

We had Coke and crisps back in the police canteen and then, when Gemma's mum had to do some work, the

Inspector took us to see a great big police dog. Gemma didn't like him and Vincent was a bit worried, but Sara laughed and patted him.

'Yes, nice doggy,' said the Inspector.

'Nice Dad-Dad,' said Sara.

She's dead artful, my little baby sister. Like I said, she insisted on staying with the Inspector, even when he had to parade some policemen and inspect some prisoners in the cells. Sara smiled all the time and the policemen and even the prisoners smiled back.

Gemma and Vincent were both getting a bit restless – and baby Clive was very restless indeed. I was tempted to leave him in one of the prisoners' cells, but one of the canteen ladies plucked him up in her arms and started cooing at him. She gave him a little lick of her special syrup pudding and it sweetened him up considerably.

I left Clive with the canteen lady
and played prisoners with Gemma
and Vincent, and a friendly policeman showed me how to take their
fingerprints with wonderful gungy
black ink. Vincent particularly
enjoyed the procedure. He didn't just
put his fingerprints on the pad. He
put them on his knees and his nose
and the desk and even up the wall.

The friendly policeman had to carry
him off to be scrubbed. I paraded
Gemma up and down the corridors
and into the control-room and

another friendly policeman showed
us how to work his computer so that
lots of squiggly green information
flashed up on the screen. Gemma
thought it was better than television
and sat on his lap and had a go at
pressing all the buttons herself.

I left Gemma with that friendly
policeman and went to see what my
fellow policewoman was up to. Gemma's mum was in the front office
seeing to members of the public. She
let me stand up on a box and see
to them too. We took particulars of
a stolen purse and Gemma's mum

showed me how to fill in a crime sheet. She said I did it very neatly. I think it's all the practice writing in this diary. I've been writing and writing and writing today since we got back home.

Mum's in bed. Sara's in bed too. She was still saying Dad-Dad as she drifted off to sleep. That Inspector says he's not her Dad-Dad but perhaps he could be a sort of uncle and come and visit her some time.

He's not a bit frowny and fierce when you get to know him. I think I'll maybe go and work full-time for him when I'm grown up.

# THURSDAY

Us girls didn't really stick together today. But it didn't matter. We still had a lot of fun. And Mum had another day in bed. She said if only she didn't feel ill it would be Absolute Bliss.

Vincent's mum looked as if she was undergoing Abject Torture. She came to collect us all with Vincent's dad. He was tall and twinkly and as soon as she spotted him Sara tried her Dad-Dad trick. It didn't work this time.

'*My* dad,' said Vincent fiercely, and when Sara tried to crawl up Vincent's dad's smartly suited trouser leg, Vincent gave her a shove so that she sat down with a thump. I don't think it hurt because her bottom's well padded with nappy, but she yelled a lot.

Vincent's dad just tutted, but Vincent's mum was horrified and told Vincent that he was a very naughty, unkind little boy and he mustn't push little girls over.

Vincent screwed up his face and looked as if he'd like to push his big mummy over. We all went to the railway station to catch the train to London. Vincent's mum and Vincent's dad and Vincent and Gemma and Clive and Sara and me. We had the double buggy and we'd started off with Vincent and Clive strapped in, Gemma holding Vincent's mum's hand, and me carrying Sara. Vincent's dad didn't seem too keen to hold or carry anyone so he just pushed the buggy.

Sara was very annoyed about this. It's our buggy and she decided she ought to be sitting in it. Vincent started struggling to get out of the buggy once we got on the platform, so Vincent's mum plucked him out and

popped Sara in his place. This wasn't as sensible as it seemed. Vincent shot off like a rocket up the platform to look for trains. Vincent's dad fielded him niftily but then handed him over firmly to Vincent's mum. She tried taking Clive out of the buggy this time and strapped Vincent back in beside Sara. Vincent yelled furiously and kicked out, trying to escape. He kicked Sara by accident and she screamed. Baby Clive cried too, just to be companionable.

Vincent's dad moved a few paces away and got out his newspaper.

'Aren't the babies being naughty,' said Gemma, squeezing Vincent's mum's hand.

Vincent's mum looked as if she were about to cry too.

'I can't have them creating this sort of chaos in my office,' she said anxiously.

'Don't worry. They were ever so good at the police station yesterday,' I said, trying to reassure her.

'Well, I don't know what on earth you were all up to, but my Vincent came home absolutely filthy. He left the most terrible fingermarks all over my cream upholstery. Vincent! Vincent, will you *stop* that silly screaming. And you, Sara. Is she always like this, Sadie? And why is the baby screeching his head off?' She held Clive as if he was a ticking bomb.

'Can't you stop him making such a noise?' Vincent's dad muttered from behind his newspaper.

'Honestly, what do you expect me to do?' said Vincent's mum crossly. 'Babies don't have volume control, you know.'

'He likes it if you jiggle him about a bit,' I said helpfully.

Vincent's mum jiggled Clive. Perhaps she jiggled him a jot too much. He was sick all down his front. He was sick down quite a lot of Vincent's mum's front too.

'Oh no,' said Vincent's mum, dabbing at the damp bits with a tissue.

'Pooh, he smells now,' said Gemma.

Clive revved up his crying, obviously insulted. Vincent and Sara were feeling ignored and so they yelled louder. Then the train rushed into the station and Gemma got startled and she started crying too.

All the other people on the platform scrambled to get into other carriages. Nobody seemed to want to sit with us. Vincent's dad looked as if he might get into another carriage too, but he manoeuvred the buggy on to the train while Vincent's mum and I hauled in all the babies. They all shut up when the train started, except Gemma. She decided she was

very seriously scared of trains. She had to sit on Vincent's mum's lap. Vincent's mum's skirt got very seriously creased.

'I must be mad,' she muttered distractedly. 'Why did I ever say I'd do this?'

'Because us girls have got to stick together,' I said brightly.

'That's all very well. But how can I be taken seriously as a professional working woman when I've got five frightful kids fighting in my office?' Vincent's mum wailed.

'*Four* kids,' I said indignantly. 'I'm here to help you.'

'Quite right, Sadie,' said Vincent's dad, twinkling at me over the top of his newspaper.

'You can shut up for a start,' said Vincent's mum.

'Now now. Temper temper. I don't know why you're getting in such a state. You've only got to look after the children for one measly little day,' said Vincent's dad. 'I'm sure you

can fit them into a corner of your office, give them some paper to crayon on, let them make necklaces out of paperclips— When you think about it, the average office is a wonderful playland for kids. You've just got to use your initiative.'

Vincent's mum squared her shoulders inside her smart suit.

'Well, I'm going to use my initiative right now,' she said, as the train drew into the station. 'If you think it's such a doddle then *you* look after the children.'

She opened the carriage door and was off down the platform, her high heels twinkling. We all peered after her, our mouths open. Vincent's dad's jaw was positively sagging.

'Mummy gone,' Vincent announced, in case we hadn't quite grasped the situation.

'Oh dear,' said Gemma. 'I liked that lady.'

'I don't like her at all,' said Vincent's dad. 'I can't believe this. How can she do this to me?'

'Maybe she'll be back in a minute,' I said helpfully. 'Maybe she's just giving you a little fright.'

She was succeeding too. Vincent's dad had gone pale and lost all his twinkle.

'What am I going to do?' he murmured wretchedly after I'd unloaded everyone and the buggy on to the platform and we'd stood around waiting for five or ten minutes. It was getting obvious that Vincent's mum really had scarpered.

'We'll have to go to your office,' I said. 'We'll fit into a corner, like you said. And we can crayon and I can make them all the paperclip necklaces and it'll be like a playland.'

'Playland! I want to go to playland!' said Gemma.

'Playland, playland,' said Vincent.

'Play!' said Sara.

'Pa-pa-pa,' said Clive.

'I wish I'd kept my big mouth shut,' said Vincent's dad.

He wouldn't attempt to take us to his office on the tube. He bundled us into a taxi.

'Are you a new kind of nanny, Gov?' said the taxi driver.

'Certainly not,' said Vincent's dad, struggling to keep control of his son while our Sara tore his newspaper into shreds and baby Clive yelled because he didn't know where he was going.

Gemma and I sat up straight and looked out of the windows, as good as gold.

'Is Playland nice, Sadie?' Gemma asked.

'I hope so,' I said.

Vincent's dad worked in a great glass building. His office was right at the top so we had to go up in a big lift. It went fast and we all held our tummies and sucked in air through our teeth. Even Clive stopped squawking and hissed in astonishment, not sure whether he liked this new sensation or not.

Vincent's dad worked in a great big room with huge windows.

'They don't open easily, do they?' I said. I am very responsible about child safety. Vincent's dad didn't seem to appreciate this at all.

'If they did open then I think I'd throw myself out,' he said. 'Look at them!'

Gemma and Vincent and Sara and Clive had instantly made themselves at home. They'd taken Vincent's dad at his word. It really was Playland.

Gemma had recognized the

computer on the desk and was stabbing happily and haphazardly at the buttons.

Vincent had found a fat felt-tip pen and was decorating a pile of official papers with yellow scribble.

Sara had overturned a big pot plant and was making a mud pie on the carpet.

61

Clive was lying on his back exercising his lungs, as he was still too little to play properly.

Vincent's dad groaned and called feebly for his secretary.

'I am prepared to pay you a double wage today, Karen, so long as you take these dreadful children off my hands,' he said weakly.

Karen giggled. 'Ah yes. Your wife's just sent a fax to see if the children are all right.'

'The children are fine, as you can see. I'm the one who is suffering. I'd like a black coffee and two aspirin, please.'

I helped Karen round everyone up. She took us to the typing pool. Gemma got disappointed because she thought she'd be able to paddle in this new pool, but she soon perked up when she saw all the word processors. She climbed on and off the typists' laps, playing with these lovely new machines.

All the typists made a great fuss of Vincent too. He ordered them about just like his dad. They sat him up on a desk with a pen and a memo pad and called him Sir.

They found a special job for Sara. The office paper-shredder was on the blink so they sat Sara down with all the unwanted paper and Sara tore and tore and tore it all into shreds. You could soon barely spot her under a great mound of scrumpled paper.

I palled up with the tealady and went all round the huge building with her, giving out all the cups of tea from her trolley. I could eat as many buns and biscuits as I wanted. I took Clive with me and whenever he got restless I just zapped him into a lift and took him for a quick trip up to the top and back.

When we'd finished the tea-round, the tealady took Clive over for a bit and I lay on top of the emptied tea-trolley, kicked off with my feet and went whizzing along the corridor. It

was better than the biggest skate-board. I nearly ran over Vincent's dad when he stepped out of his office but he managed to leap out of the way just in time.

He had a right cheek. Vincent's mum turned up at lunchtime, saying she'd got all her work done so she'd take us over for the afternoon. Vincent's dad acted as if he'd looked after us single-handed, and Vincent's mum said she was sorry and she thought he was splendid and when my mum was well enough to babysit she'd take him out for a slap-up meal to say thank you.

Vincent's mum took Vincent and Gemma and Clive and our Sara and me to a McDonald's for our lunch, which was great, and then she took us to a proper playground. Vincent's mum sat on a bench and did some of her paperwork while I pushed everyone on the swings and then we all sat in the sandpit and made sandcastles. Whenever anyone started crying, Vincent's mum bought ice-creams from a nearby van. We ended up having three or maybe it was four ice-creams, even Clive.

Clive wasn't the only one who was sick on the train going home.

# FRIDAY

Mum's a bit better. She was worried when she heard about the argy-bargy between Vincent's mum and Vincent's dad.

'I think I'd better get back to looking after all the children today,' Mum said, and she got up for breakfast.

'Oh Mum, don't be silly. You still seem very fluey to me,' I said.

'I certainly *look* a bit fluey,' said Mum, running her fingers through her straggly hair and rubbing her poor red nose. 'But I still think it's time I took over. It sounds as if you're all running wild.'

'Grrr,' I said, baring my teeth and making my hands into claws.

'Grrr,' Sara copied, biting her breakfast banana very savagely.

'Anyway, Mum, you can't take over today. We'll miss out on all the fun,' I said tactlessly. 'I can't wait to go to Clive's mum's chocolate shop. Yum yum yum.'

'Yum yum,' said Sara, slobbering.

'Yes, that's what I'm worried about,' said Mum. 'Sara was sick yesterday. I don't want her eating lots of chocolate today and getting sick again.'

'It's OK, Mum. I'll look after her. I'm the mum-minder now and I'm supposed to be looking after you. So you go back to bed. You look all white and wobbly.'

'I do feel a bit shaky. All right then, Sadie.'

'That's a good mum,' I said. 'Back to bed. I'll come and tuck you up in a minute.'

We both giggled because every-thing was back to front and it sounded so funny, me telling Mum what to do. I don't want Mum to stay ill, but I wish I could always boss her around!

Clive's mum could do with being a bit bossier. She's little, not all that much bigger than me, and I bet I weigh more. I know if I worked in a chocolate shop I'd grow very big indeed. It's such a wonderful shop. Just the rich, creamy, chocolaty smell makes your mouth start water-ing. Clive's mum showed us all round the big glass cabinets piled high with hazelnut truffles and white whirly creams, strawberry marzipans and violet fondants, sugar mice and chocolate teddies.

'Can I have a chocolate teddy?' Gemma asked, reaching out.

'Chocolate ted!' Vincent demanded, grabbing.

'Choc choc!' said Sara, scrabbling.

'No, wait a minute! You mustn't touch, dears. Gemma, put it down, darling. Vincent, no! And look at Sara, she's dribbling all over the display,' said Clive's mum, dashing from one to the other.

Clive decided he wanted his mum's attention for himself.

'Oh dear. I don't know why he's crying, he's only just had his bottle,' said Clive's mum. 'Look, Gemma dear, I don't really think your mummy would like you to have *another* chocolate teddy. Vincent, don't touch those chocolate boxes! Oh

dear, Sara. No, poppet, take it out of your mouth.'

I sussed out a stock-room at the back, with big empty cardboard boxes. I grabbed Sara and Gemma and lifted them into one box. It was more of a struggle with Vincent, but I eventually seized hold of him under the armpits and hauled him into the back room and caged him in another cardboard box.

'You're all wild animals in the zoo,' I said quickly. 'And it's feeding time. I'm the keeper and I've just fed you, right? You've got to growl back at me, grrrr, grrrr.'

'Grrr,' said Sara, who was used to this game.

Luckily, Gemma and Vincent thought it was fun too. They gnawed their stolen chocolate and growled contentedly. Clive did his best to play, roaring magnificently. He was a little too young for a cardboard cage and he was only allowed the merest lick of chocolate, so I carried him round and round the shop to quieten him down.

'You're such a good girl, Sadie. You've got them all sorted out in no time,' said Clive's mum gratefully. 'Here, you'd better help yourself to a chocolate too.'

I rather hoped she'd offer me one. I wanted to show how grown up I am so I tried a liqueur chocolate. I was a bit disappointed in the taste. I hoped I'd get drunk. I started swaying about the shop experimentally and baby Clive chuckled, enjoying getting jiggled around. I decided to sober up, because I remembered what happened if you jiggled him too much. I

also knew we couldn't let the children chomp chocolate all day long. When the wild animals finished feeding and started to get so restless they were breaking right out of their cages, I offered to take them for a walk on the common.

Clive's mum said she thought this was a wonderful idea but she didn't see how I could manage all the babies by myself. I suggested putting the two littlest in the double buggy and tying Vincent and Gemma with chocolate-box ribbon like a lead. Clive's mum

still looked doubtful, but then Clive's granny came into the shop to see how she was coping.

'I'll take little Clive off your hands for an hour or so,' she offered.

'We could all go for a walk together,' I suggested.

'Oh no, dear, I don't think that's a good idea,' said Clive's granny quickly, but she wasn't quick enough.

'Let's go for a walk,' said Gemma, holding out her sticky hand.

'Me want to go for a run,' said Vincent, already at the door.

'Walk! Run!' Sara insisted.

Clive joined in the general uproar, telling his granny that he wanted his friends to go with him.

She was stuck with us. She didn't really *do* anything. She just pushed the buggy while I kept tight hold of Gemma and Vincent, and then when we got to the common she sat on a bench with Clive perched on her knee.

'You're free for a bit, wild animals,' I said, letting them go.

Gemma growled her way through the jungly bushes. Vincent galloped over the plain. Sara stalked prey in the undergrowth. They made a lot of wild animal noises. So did Clive. His granny bounced him up and down on her knee. She bounced him a bit too vigorously. I helped her mop him up. Then I rounded up all my wild animals. That took quite a time. I had to wrestle with them before they would submit. But at last I got them all reasonably tamed and we trailed back to the shop.

Clive's gran said she was exhausted and she'd have to go home for a lie down. Clive's mum and I had a little giggle about her after she'd gone. Then we gave the littlest wild animal his bottle, and fed the others on Marmite sandwiches and crisps and carrots and orange juice. They'd already had more than enough chocolate.

I still felt I hadn't had quite *enough* chocolate. I hadn't rudely grabbed for myself like the little kids, and the chocolate liqueur had come as a bit of a disappointment. I thought about this rather wistfully as I helped change and pot the wild animals (not yet properly house-trained) and then settled them down in their cardboard cages for a nap. All that running wild seemed to have tired them out. They were all fast asleep within five minutes.

I tiptoed out of the stock-room to join Clive's mum. There was a chocolate heart waiting for me on the counter. It had a special message in

swirly pink icing: *Thank you, Sadie!*

I said a lot of thank-yous back and ate it all up. It tasted wonderful.

Clive's mum showed me how to write swirly messages myself using the icing bag. I practised on a paper bag at first because my writing went a bit haywire, but when I'd got the knack she let me write my own message on a heart: *Get well soon, Mum.*

'Ah, that's lovely,' said Clive's mum. 'Yes, I think we're all wishing that, Sadie.'

# SATURDAY

My chocolate heart worked. Mum is very nearly better. Nan's getting better too and says she'll be back to help Mum on Monday. When I told her how I'd been mum-minding she said I was a Little Treasure. Grandad said I was too. He says he's still feeling poorly. Nan says he just wants to lie back in bed and be waited on hand and foot, and he isn't half getting on her nerves.

Mum and I are getting on just great. Saturdays are good anyway

because the dads take over the babies. Our dad doesn't often come for Sara and me, but that doesn't matter. Us girls stick together.

We all had a bit of a lie in and then I got up and made tea and toast, and Sara and I got in Mum's bed and we had breakfast together. It got a bit crumby but it was very cosy all the same.

Then I got Sara sorted out and put her in her playpen.

Then I got Mum sorted out too. I poured lots of bubbles in the bath and she lay back in it like a film star and then I helped her wash her hair. We played hairdressers after, and I did her hair in all different daft styles, and then Sara wanted to join in, even though she's just got these little feathery curls that stick straight up in the air. Clive's mum had given me some of the chocolate-box ribbon so I tied a blue bow round Sara's biggest

80

curl, and she chuckled when she saw herself in the mirror.

Then Mum brushed her hair out into her own proper style and got dressed and put some powder on her poor sore nose so that it didn't look so red.

'There! I look a new woman,' said Mum. 'I think I'm up to a little outing.'

We went down to the shopping centre, the three of us. I made Mum wrap up really warm with an extra jumper and a scarf. We had a morning coffee together, with Danish pastries, one each. Sara just sucked the jam off

hers but she enjoyed it a lot, so it
wasn't wasted. She was quite happy
swinging her legs in the roomy buggy
and licking her lips while Mum and I
sat and chatted like grown-up ladies.
Then we went round the shops for a
bit, looking at all the toys and clothes
and choosing what we'd buy if we had
all the money in the world. But then

Mum got a bit tired so we caught the bus home.

I put Sara down for her nap.

I put Mum down for a nap and all.

Then I did a bit of tidying and swept the floor and stuffed some things in the washing machine. A woman's work is never done. Ha ha.

Mum was ever so pleased when she woke up. She gave me the rest of her *Get Well Soon, Mum* chocolate heart. She'd only had two bites. She still hasn't got her appetite back, but she

really is practically better. She says I've been the best mum-minder in the whole world.

Mum did the ironing herself this evening because I get things a bit scrumpled when I have a go. But I put Sara to bed. I read her *Dominic the Vole*. Some of the words are missing where she's had another savage gnaw, but it doesn't matter. I have

read *Dominic the Vole* at least one hundred times and I know it off by heart.

Then when Sara was settled, I read to Mum while she ironed. I read her this holiday diary and she didn't half laugh.

# SUNDAY

This isn't just a holiday diary. It's a huge great blockbusting *book*. I ought to get a gold star for extra effort at the very least (hint hint). Maybe I ought to be a writer when I grow up. Though I think I'd sooner have my own chocolate shop. I'd still like to be a policewoman too. And you get lots of money if you work in an office, so that you can buy ten or twenty ice-creams on the trot without fussing. But I know one thing. I'm never going to be a childminder.

I've done enough of that to last me six
centuries.

I've finished being a mum-minder
too. My mum's completely better.

She took Sara and me to the Leisure Centre this afternoon. It was absolutely great. Rachel from up the road was there too, and we went in the big pool and splashed in the fountains and screamed non-stop when they switched the big wave on. Mum went in the baby's pool with Sara. Sara splashed and screamed a lot too, and kicked her fat little feet about. I played with her for a bit while Mum had a swim. I swooped her up and down so she had her own little wave. She didn't half like that.

But after a bit she started to get shivery. So did I. So we all got out

and Mum wrapped us both in big towels and then when we were dry and dressed we went and had a hot chocolate in the cafe. (Sara just had a teaspoon of froth off the top.)

Funny though. I still couldn't get properly warm. Sara started sneezing on the way home.

'Oh no,' said Mum. 'Don't say Sara's got my flu. Poor little poppet.'

Then I sneezed six times without stopping.

'Oh no,' said Mum again.

'Oh yes,' I said. 'Poor little Sadie!'

'Poor little me,' said Mum. 'It looks like I'm going to have my hands full nursing you two.'

'Let's hope Gemma and Vincent and baby Clive haven't caught it too. Then it won't just be your hands — you'll have two arms and a leg full as well,' I said.

*Later*
I am still sneezing. I am still shivery. My head hurts. I do not feel very well at all. I think I definitely do have flu. I am not pleased. Although wait a minute. If I've got flu I won't be able to go back to school tomorrow. So I'll have more holiday, even though it looks like I'll be stuck in bed.

*Later still*
If I don't go back to school tomorrow I won't be able to hand in my holiday diary. So what does that mean? I've filled up all this great long book for nothing!

# THE END

## ABOUT THE AUTHOR

JACQUELINE WILSON is one of Britain's most outstanding writers for young readers. She is the most borrowed author from British libraries and has sold over 25 million books in this country. As a child, she always wanted to be a writer and wrote her first 'novel' when she was nine, filling countless exercise books as she grew up. She started work at a publishing company and then went on to work as a journalist on *Jackie* magazine (which was named after her) before turning to writing fiction full-time.

Jacqueline has been honoured with many of the UK's top awards for children's books, including the Guardian Children's Fiction Award, the Smarties Prize, the Red House Book Award and the Children's Book of the Year. She was awarded an OBE in 2002 and was the Children's Laureate for 2005-2007.

## ABOUT THE ILLUSTRATOR

NICK SHARRATT knew from an early age that he wanted to use his drawing skills as his career, so he went to Manchester Polytechnic to do an Art Foundation course. He followed this up with a BA (Hons) in Graphic Design at St. Martin's School of Art in London from 1981–1984.

Since graduating, Nick has been working full-time as an illustrator for children's books, publishers and a wide range of magazines. His brilliant illustrations have brought to life many books, most notably the titles by Jacqueline Wilson.

Nick also writes books as well as illustrating them.

# SLEEPOVERS
Jacqueline Wilson

**Sleepover parties are the greatest!**
**Everybody's having one . . .**

All of Daisy's friends in the Alphabet Club – Amy,
Bella, Chloe and Emily, have had sleepovers for their
birthdays. Daisy has a dilemma. She'd love to have a
sleepover too, but then she'd have to let her
friends meet her sister...

A funny and moving story for younger readers
from the award-winning author of *Lizzie Zipmouth*
and *Double Act*.

ISBN: 978 0 552 55783 2

# THE WORRY WEBSITE
## Jacqueline Wilson

**Type in your worry . . .**

Is anything bothering you? Problems in class or
at home? Don't know where to turn for help?
Log on to the Worry Website! Type in your worry
and wait for the good advice to flow in.

At least that's the plan when Mr Speed sets up his
super-cool new Worry Website for the class. Holly,
Greg, Natasha and the rest feel that they've got
shedloads of worries but, as they find out,
sometimes the best advice comes from the most
unexpected place.

A fabulous collection of linked short stories from the
bestselling, award-winning Jacqueline Wilson.
Also includes a prize-winning story by a
12-year-old writer!

ISBN: 978 0 440 86826 2

# The Mum-Minder

I wonder if you used to be looked afte[r]
child-minder while your mum went out to
Or maybe, like Sadie in this book, your mi
a child-minder herself? I think child-min[der]
do a wonderful job, but there's always the
problem. What happens when the child-mi[nder]
gets ill? Who gets to look after all the babies?

I heard a bunch of young mums discussin[g]
one day at a party and decided that this migh[t]
a good funny story. I had great fun inven[ting]
the different naughty little children – and
Nick's baby drawings are superb. I espe[cially]
the way he draws babies' hair with those
bits on top (I have a similar hairstyle!)

used to have a friend called Dominic who
ot begging me to put him into one of my
ildren's books.

"Go on, Jacky,' he'd say. 'I could be an animal
you like. I could be Dominic the Dragon or
Dominic the Dinosaur. Or I could be just a little
tiny sweet shy animal – Dominic the Vole?"

So Sadie's little sister, Sara, loves her picture book
*Dominic the Vole* and poor Sadie has to read it to her
over and over again. I think Sadie's mum is very
lucky to have such a kind helpful daughter.

*Jacqueline Wilson*

# Which Jacqueline Wilson characters have you met already?

## Sadie

Sadie's mum is a child-minder and she often helps out. But things go wrong when her mum gets ill and Sadie has to be a mum-minder *and* a stand-in child-minder! Find out all about Sadie in **The Mum Minder.**

## Daisy

Daisy is part of the Alphabet club with her friends Amy, Bella, Chloe and Emily. They're all having sleepovers for their birthdays and Daisy's not sure she wants one. Find out why and meet Daisy in **Sleepovers.**

## Lizzie

Lizzie's been happy living with her mum. But now Mum insists that they move in with her new partner and his sons. Lizzie is not pleased so she stops speaking. Will stubborn Lizzie keep her silence up? Find out and meet Lizzie in **Lizzie Zipmouth.**

## Verity

Verity's really upset when her cat Mabel dies. Then she finds out about the ancient Egyptians and decides to make Mabel into a cat-mummy. Will it work? Find out more about Verity in **The Cat Mummy.**

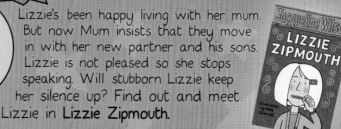

If you like this book, you'll love meeting these girls too!

# Jacqueline

# The Mum-Minder

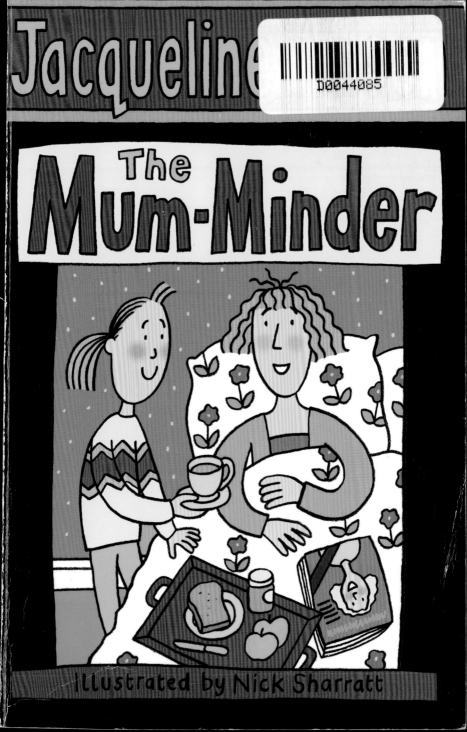

Illustrated by Nick Sharratt